THE LION KING

As the morning sun rose high over the African plain, animals and birds gathered at the foot of Pride Rock. This was a very special day!

They watched in silence as Rafiki, a wise old baboon, raised a lion cub high in the air. The clouds parted and the sun's rays shone down on the new Prince—Prince Simba, the future king.

Slowly Rafiki lowered his arms and took Simba back to his proud parents, King Mufasa and Queen Sarabi.

Simba grew into a playful, curious cub. One morning, Mufasa explained to him, "Everything the light touches is our kingdom. One day, Simba, the sun will set on my time here, and will rise with you as the new king. We are all connected in the great Circle of Life."

Later that day, Simba bragged to his Uncle Scar that he had seen the whole of his future kingdom.

"Even beyond the northern border?" Scar asked slyly.

"Well, no," said Simba sadly. "He said I can't go there."

"And he's absolutely right," said Scar. "Only the *bravest* lions go there. An elephant graveyard is no place for a young prince."

Simba didn't see his uncle's evil trap. He decided to show his father what a brave cub he could be.

Simba set out to find his best friend, Nala, and visit the elephant graveyard that very day. He had no idea that Scar had ordered three hyenas to go to the elephant graveyard, too, to kill the cub— as part of his plan to take over Mufasa's kingdom!

Simba raced ahead across the plains, leading
Nala to the forbidden place. Eventually they
reached a pile of elephant bones.

"It's really creepy," said Nala.

Simba was about to explore a skull,
when he saw Zazu, his father's adviser.

Zazu commanded them to leave
immediately, saying, "You are in very
real danger."

But it was too late! They were
trapped by three laughing, drooling
hyenas!

Simba took a deep breath and tried
to roar—but only a squeaky rumble
came out. The hyenas laughed even
more.

Simba took another deep breath.

"ROAARR!" The hyenas looked
around into the eyes of—King Mufasa!
They fled howling into the mist.

Mufasa scolded his son on the way home. "You deliberately disobeyed me."

"I was just trying to be brave, like you," said Simba softly.

"Being brave doesn't mean you go looking for trouble," replied Mufasa.

The moon shone brightly above them and the stars twinkled in the dark sky.

Mufasa stopped. "Look at the stars! The great kings of the past look down on us from those stars. So, whenever you feel alone, just remember that those kings will always be there to guide you, and so will I."

Meanwhile, Scar came up with a new plan. He led Simba down a steep gorge and told him to wait for his father. Then the hyenas started a stampede among a herd of wildebeests, rushing them through the gorge toward Simba!

Mufasa heard the thunder of hooves and raced to the rescue.

"Hold on, Simba!" he cried.

The king rescued his son, but he could
not save himself. He fell back onto an
overhanging rock. Looking up, he saw
his brother.

"Scar, help me!" he cried. But Scar
pushed Mufasa into the path of
the trampling wildebeests.

When the stampede was over, Simba
ran to his father's side.

"Dad," he whimpered, nuzzling
Mufasa's mane. But the king did not reply.
Simba started sobbing.

"Simba," said Scar coldly, "what have
you done? The king is dead, and if it
weren't for you, he'd still be alive. Run
away, Simba. Run away and never return."

As Scar returned to take the royal
throne at Pride Rock for himself, Simba
stumbled, exhausted and frightened,
through the grasslands toward the jungle.
He finally collapsed. Hungry vultures
circled above him.

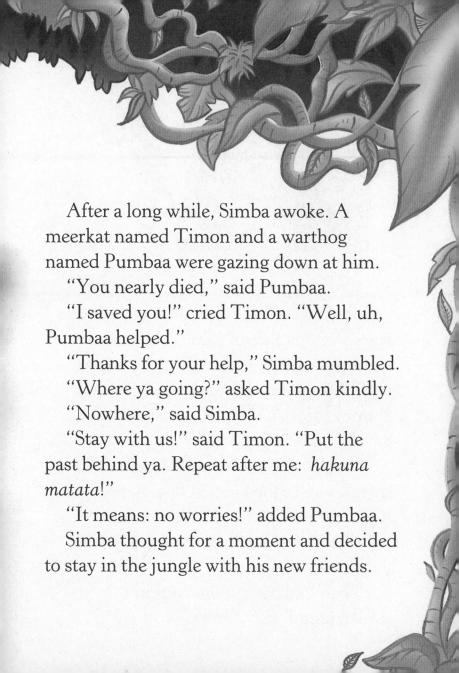

After a long while, Simba awoke. A meerkat named Timon and a warthog named Pumbaa were gazing down at him.

"You nearly died," said Pumbaa.

"I saved you!" cried Timon. "Well, uh, Pumbaa helped."

"Thanks for your help," Simba mumbled.

"Where ya going?" asked Timon kindly.

"Nowhere," said Simba.

"Stay with us!" said Timon. "Put the past behind ya. Repeat after me: *hakuna matata!*"

"It means: no worries!" added Pumbaa.

Simba thought for a moment and decided to stay in the jungle with his new friends.

Many years later, deep in a cave, Rafiki stared at a picture of a lion. "It is time," he said, smiling, and prepared to leave.

The very next day, Simba rescued Pumbaa from a hungry lioness—and it was Nala, his old friend!

"You're alive!" she said happily. "That means you're the king!" Nala told Simba how Scar had destroyed the Pride Lands. "Simba, if you don't do something, soon everyone will starve."

"I can't go back. You wouldn't understand," said Simba.

Nala was disappointed in her friend.
"Don't *you* understand? You're our
only hope."

Nala turned and left her friend alone.

That night, Simba lay by a stream, thinking.
He heard a noise and looked up. It was Rafiki.
"I know your father," said Rafiki. "I'll show
him to you. You follow Rafiki. Come on."

Simba followed Rafiki in wonder to the edge of the stream. As Simba looked into the water, his reflection changed shape and became his father's! He heard Mufasa's voice:

"Simba. Remember who you are. You are my son and the one true king." Then the reflection and Rafiki disappeared.

"I must return," decided Simba.

Meanwhile, back at the Pride Lands, storm clouds had gathered and a lightning bolt scorched the earth. As the dry grasses caught fire, huge flames swept toward Pride Rock—and a lion appeared through the smoke.

It was Simba!

Scar lunged at Simba, determined to kill him just as he had Mufasa. Timon and Pumbaa joined in the fierce battle that followed, as lionesses drove back the hyenas. Simba finally heaved Scar over a cliff. Scar landed—to find himself surrounded by drooling hyenas.

Simba was victorious!

Nala went to Simba's side. "Welcome home," she whispered.

Simba took his rightful place as the Lion King, and once again the land flourished. The plains came back to life and the herds returned.